Once, I Laughed My Socks Off

Poems for kids

Steve Attewell

www.laughedmysocksoff.com

Cover art by Simon Oxley

ISBN-13: 978-1475030457
ISBN-10: 1475030452

DEDICATION

To my brother, without whom growing up wouldn't have been half-as-much fun.

CONTENTS

Once, I laughed my socks off

Once, I laughed my socks off,
And they ran off down the street,
I caught them, but they wouldn't let me,
Put them on my feet,

They danced around behind me,
As I made my way back home,
They jumped and jived about the place,
They'd not leave me alone,

I went into the living room,
To sit and watch T.V.,
But they danced around in front of me;
I couldn't see the screen,

I tried to do the washing up,
But much to my surprise,
They jumped around inside the bowl,
And splashed me in the eyes,

"Oh socks," I said, "do please give up,
This dancing to and fro,
Not least because it was that I,
Stopped laughing hours ago!"

They looked forlorn, those socks of mine,
Accepting their defeat,
They sidled to the side of me,
And slipped back on my feet,

Next time I laugh, I will ensure,
My shoes are firmly on,
That should stop my naughty socks,
From such a carry-on.

Melvin the naughty teddy bear

Melvin was a naughty bear,
Did naughty things, not least,
When he'd sneak down to the fridge,
To grab a midnight feast,

He'd eat all last night's chicken,
And scoff down all the cheese,
"This is fun, it's great," he thought,
"This is a jolly wheeze."

One night he ate some mouldy cheese,
That was a little runny,
He felt quite ill, but still he ate,
His tummy felt quite funny,

He thought a mushroom might just help,
And munched through nine or ten,
That just made him feel much worse,
How can we solve this then?

"Maybe jelly'd fix my belly,
Or maybe fruit or beans!"
He ate the lot, he couldn't stop,
Then found some custard creams,

"Might a biscuit make me feel,
A great deal better soon?"
He ate them, but they didn't,
So he grabbed the largest spoon,

"I'll dig into this custard then,"
Thought Melvin with a smile,
He spilt the custard on his paws,
Grinning all the while,

He searched through all the kitchen drawers,
To find the jam and honey,
And after he ate both of those,
His tummy *still* felt funny,

He said, "I'll have some toasted bread,
Washed down with lemonade,"
And carried on regardless with,
His naughty escapade,

Then he stopped; the buttons popped,
Upon his little shirt,
"Time for bed," he thought,
"There is no room for my dessert!"

He tried to move, but thus he proved,
Too big to pass the door,
And so, he settled down to sleep,
Upon the kitchen floor,

Next morning down came Alice,
(The girl that owned the bear),
She spied the smears upon the walls,
The mess was everywhere,

"Melvin bear what have you done?
You should be up in bed,"
She searched around and found him down,
Beneath a pile of bread,

"I haven't eaten anything!"
Said Melvin with a grin,
While wiping crumbs from off his shirt,
And jam from off his chin,

"Don't lie," said Alice scornfully,
"The evidence is clear,
There are jammy paw prints on the floor,
Look here, and here, and here,"

Melvin wrung his sticky paws,
It's proof, no doubt of that,
Then he felt quite queasy,
And was sick upon the mat,

"Oh, I don't feel well," he said,
"I won't do this again,
I promise no more midnight feasts,
I really will refrain,"

Alice took him up to bed,
And mopped his sweaty brow,
"You ate so much, you're feeling ill,
You're paying for it now!"

And so it was that Melvin stayed,
In bed for three more days,
He felt so ill, he promised to,
Forever change his ways,

He was careful with his cup cakes,
Hardly had much ham,
And sensible with sandwiches,
But still ate too much jam.

Bingo the Boo

"Nick nacky nack noo!"
Sang Bingo the Boo,
A Boo is a creature invisible to you,

But sometimes at night,
I see him take flight,
And loop-the-loop all round my room,

His head is bright blue,
And his body is too,
His feet big and red like a clown,

He takes great delight,
In things sparkly and bright,
And sometimes flies right upside-down,

He stretches his wings,
And swoops around things,
Round my bed, round my chair, and my lamp

He shot through the door,
Scooped my socks from the floor,
And ate them, the naughty young scamp

He tried to then flee,
But knocked over my tea,
He's a cheeky thing I must confess,

When I look at the state,
Of my bedroom of late,
I survey such a terrible mess,

If it wasn't for he,
Clean, my room it would be,
I must tidy and dust and vacuum,

Now you've nothing to fear,
But I hope you don't hear,
Bingo sing, "Nick nacky nack noo."

Daddy's accident

Daddy he had a knee,
Hurt a knee painfully,
How can we fix a knee hurting like that?

He wrenched and he twist it,
He slipped on a biscuit,
And tripped and fell over the cat,

Said the vet: "See your pet?
A crash hat needs your cat,
See this bump, this big lump on his head?"

"I'm no good with knees,
Pets are my expertise,
And your cat needs a long rest in bed."

Daddy and cat,
Took the longest of naps,
Following doctor's advice to the letter,

And then by the morning,
The both of them yawning,
They both felt a little bit better,

So don't leave your biscuits,
And trinkets and such,
On carpet or rug upon floor,

'Cos trinkets and biscuits,
Are slipped on and tripped on,
Tidy floors are just safe all the more.

Ebb and Flo

"Look out below!" cried out Flo,
"I'm coming in to land,"
She flapped and wavered, in the air,
Landing not quite how she'd planned,

She bumped into the other dove,
Knocking him right over,
"What's this?" thought Ebb, he rubbed his head,
Spread-eagled in the clover,

He'd hit the ground and lay face down,
Dazed amongst the daisies,
He pulled his beak out of the lawn,
"Someone must be crazy!"

He looked above, and saw a dove,
As beautiful as spring,
Flo looked down, embarrassed,
And she offered him a wing,

Gratefully he took it,
And she helped him to his feet,
She dust him down, and cooed,
"I only came from 'cross the street,"

"I saw you here, and thought to come,
and say a quick 'hello',
A gust of wind, it caught my wing,
And blew me to and fro."

"You caught me by surprise," said Ebb,
"I wondered: 'What was that?',
'Who knocked me to the ground?' I thought,
It might have been a cat,"

"There's one that prowls the garden,
And I've had a few close calls,
I lost some feathers, to him once,
I don't like him at all."

"I'm no beastly pet, no threat,
There's no misunderstanding,"
Said Flo, "I'm just a normal dove,
My landings notwithstanding."

Said Ebb, "A dove? A bird thereof?
One mastered in her flight?"
Said Flo, "I fly, I flap my wings,
But 'mastered'? Well, not quite."

Flo looked sad, she'd never told,
How hard she found her flying,
"I'm not the best, I must confess,
But not for lack of trying."

Remembering the teases that,
She'd heard at flying school,
Her agitated feathers flapped,
She felt like such a fool,

Flo turned away, embarrassed,
With a tear upon her cheek,
She felt abashed, to blurt out that,
At which she was so weak,

Ebb chirped, "It's okay, I'll help."
He was happy, and up-beat,
He placed his wing upon her back,
Flo said, "That's very sweet."

"I've tried and tried, it does no good,
to labor on the fact,
That I'm no good at flying and so,
That, I say, is that!"

Sullenly, she turned and flew,
Unsteadily, she stalled,
Then faltered o'er the flower beds,
And hit the garden wall,

Dashing over in a flash,
Ebb glided to her side,
She lay amongst the roses,
Petals scattered far and wide,

He pecked a petal from Flo's head,
Revealing eyes a-glazed,
Flo blinked, and then, expound a frown,
Awaking from her daze,

"Where am I, who are you?" she asked,
His eyes were all aglow,
"Pleased to meet you, my name's Ebb."
She smiled, "Hello, I'm Flo."

"Are you hurt?" asked Ebb, concerned,
"Can you wiggle everything?"
"My legs are fine, my tail's okay,"
She winced, "I've hurt my wing."

Flo's wing was caught upon the thorns,
It bled and stained her red,
She lay there lame, and then there came,
A shadow overhead.

Atop the wall the cat looked down,
At Ebb and Flo below,
Ebb took flight, "Let's go, alight!"
Stuck fast in thorns was Flo,

The cat jumped down and crouched to ground,
And wiggled its behind,
It twitched an ounce, and thought to pounce,
Upon its lucky find,

Its eyes fixed fast upon our Flo,
And hers upon the cat,
The dreadful wait seemed endless,
She thought, "That, may well, be that."

"Here I am, alone," she cooed,
"Ebb's nowhere to be seen,
My only hope, has flown away,"
But if her eyes had been more keen,

She would have spied, high in the sky,
A dot approaching fast,
Diving though the air above,
Its speed was unsurpassed,

Ebb tucked his wings against himself,
Air pummelling his face,
Dove directly at the cat,
And quickened up his pace,

The cat sprang forth, toward its prey,
And Flo curled up in fear,
But at that moment Ebb shot down,
A dove-shaped bombardier,

He hit the cat square in the back,
And knocked it to the ground,
A mess of fur and feathers flew,
All full of screeching sounds,

The cat sprang ten feet in the air,
Its tail a bristled brush,
It ran to house, fast though its flap,
Leaving naught but dust,

Ebb helped Flo up to her feet,
"We mustn't stick around,
That lousy cat, it might be back."
With that, they left the ground.

Said Ebb, "Stop flapping randomly,
Relax and feel the beat,
Your legs are running in the air!
Tuck in those little feet."

They struggled off to safety,
Away, for peace to find,
Ebb disappeared behind the wall,
Flo flapping fast behind,

A year had passed and I was lazing,
Sun-kissed out the back,
When, two collared doves appeared,
Both soared with quite a knack,

They skimmed across the garden wall,
And loop-the-looped, before,
Deftly landing on the lawn,
Followed by two more,

Smaller were the second pair,
Fledgling kids I think,
Flitting 'bout the birdbath,
Stopping often there to drink,

The cat, it never bothers them,
It never bats an eye,
It sneaks a peak, but turns its tail,
No excited battle cry,

The larger doves, sit close and watch,
They look like friends forever,
I see them swoop through summer skies,
And ebb and flow together.

Desmond the fairy

Desmond the fairy is green and quite hairy,
But that's not a bad thing you see,
Because Desmond's quite shy, and this is no lie,
He hides in your Christmas tree,

If you half close your eyes and look into the tree,
You may see him prancing around gleefully,
He'll swoop down in a crescent to check all the presents,
And he polishes baubles for free,

Desmond will squeak if his interest is piqued,
By a present that's wonderfully huge,
He'll jump up and down, and run all around,
And turn from a green to a rouge,

Once, so excited and happy, delighted,
He cackled and cooed and he crowed,
He shook and vibrated, he was so elated,
Which caused him to pop and explode,

So the Fairy King came and brought him to life,
He chanted and threw fairy dust,
Desmond said, "Thanks, can I do that again?"
And the king replied, "Well, if you must."

The Fairy King knew that some fairies are bonkers,
Batty and crazed and berserk,
But nothing, not popping, expiring or tiring,
Should ever stop one from their work,

If on Christmas Eve you take leave to perceive,
A rustling and twitching of tree,
That could be Desmond a-dancing and prancing,
And polishing baubles for free.

Trees are good

Trees are good,
They're made of wood,
And suck up CO^2,

They process, then,
Give oxygen,
That's air for me and you,

So treat a tree,
With respect, you see,
They help us every day,

You mightn't believe,
They help us breathe,
But they're good for sticks anyway.

Steve Attewell

ABOUT THE AUTHOR

Steve Attewell was born in the sleepy village of Fair Oak in the south of England in the peak of the long, hot summer of 1975. He thinks this might be why he doesn't like the cold very much. His first published book of amusing poetry for kids is "Once, I Laughed My Socks Off".

www.laughedmysocksoff.com

CPSIA information can be obtained
at www.ICGtesting.com
Printed in the USA
BVHW040201060520
579282BV00014B/549

9 781475 030457